New Shoes, Red Shoes

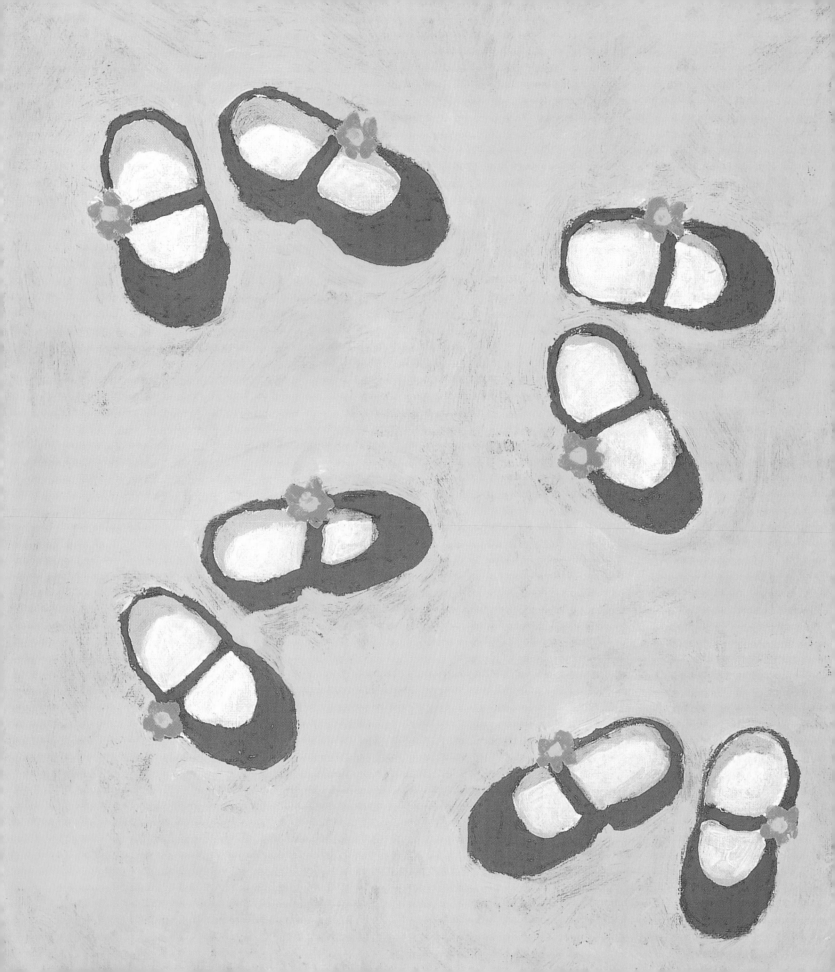

For Christine—
special friends are always treasured.

ISBN 0-439-35864-7

Copyright © 2000 by Susan Rollings. All rights reserved.
Published by Scholastic Inc., 555 Broadway, New York, NY 10012,
by arrangement with Orchard Books, Inc.
SCHOLASTIC and associated logos are trademarks and/or registered
trademarks of Scholastic Inc.

12 11 10 9 8 7 6 5 4 3 2   1 2 3 4 5 6/0

Printed in the U.S.A.   14

First Scholastic printing, February 2001

The text of this book is set in 60 point Blockhead Unplugged.
The illustrations are gouache.

New Shoes, Red Shoes

Susan Rollings

SCHOLASTIC INC.
New York Toronto London Auckland Sydney
Mexico City New Delhi Hong Kong

Two shoes,
small shoes.

Off to get some
new shoes.

Low shoes, high shoes.

Sitting on the bus shoes.

Flat shoes,
summer shoes.

Friends with
very pointy shoes.

Warm shoes,
        soft shoes.

Tiny little baby shoes.

Tired shoes,
        dirty shoes.

Rows and rows
and rows of shoes.

Blue shoes,
    pink shoes.

Red and shiny
        new shoes.

Best shoes,
    special shoes.

Home with
very precious shoes.

New shoes,
   party shoes.

Time to put them on shoes.

Happy shoes,
dancing shoes.

Skipping to the
party shoes.

Ribbon shoes,
sparkly shoes.

Big and
    noisy racing shoes.

Magic shoes,
disco shoes.

Mustn't step on
these new shoes.

Lots and lots
and lots of shoes.

But best of all
are MY shoes!

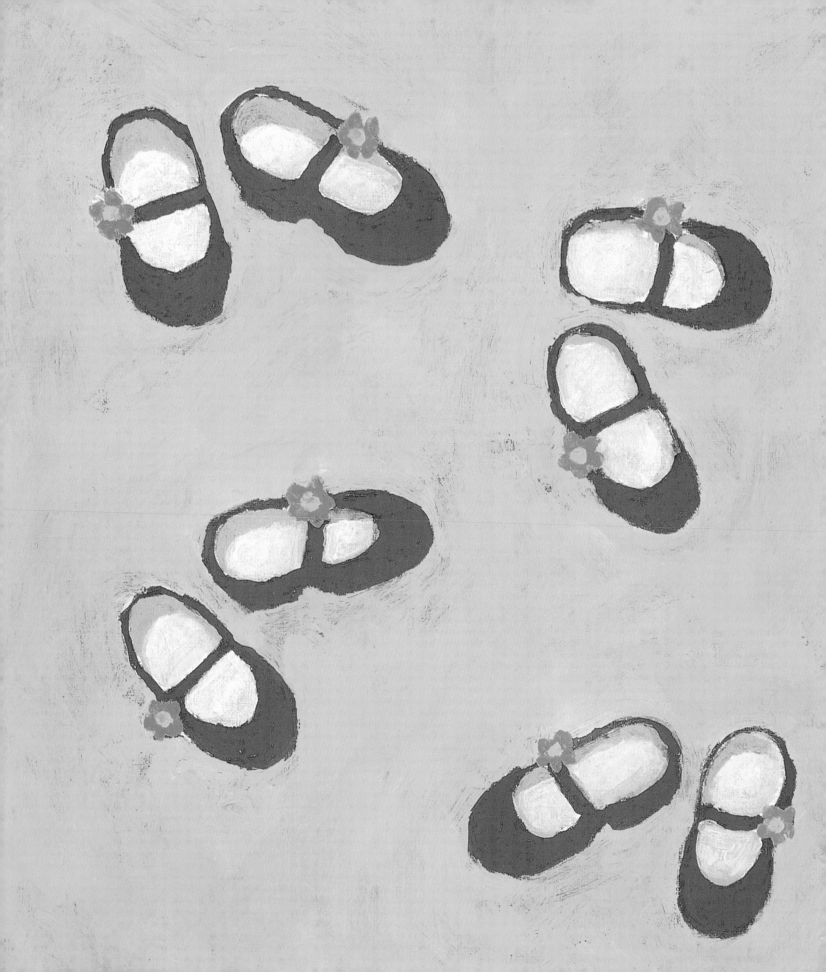